Ish River

POEMS BY ROBERT SUND

NORTH POINT PRESS

San Francisco 1983

The poems in Book One were published in a letterpress
limited edition from Copper Canyon Press, Port Town-
send, Washington. Some of the poems were previously
published in magazines, newsletters, and broadsides,
including *Kuksu, The Arts, Double Elephant, Kee Yoks,*
and others.

In memory of
my father and mother,
my grandfather and grandmother
Evart and Elsa, Johan and Ida
Sund

Contents

Preface

"Ish River"—
  like breath,
  like mist rising from a hillside.
Duwamish, Snohomish, Stillaguamish, Samish,
Skokomish, Skykomish . . . all the ish rivers.

I live in the Ish River country
between two mountain ranges where
many rivers
run down to an inland sea.

     R. S.
     March 29, 1979
     Cloud House

Book 1

The Hides of White Horses Shedding Rain

Night along the Columbia, Day in Blewett Pass, Going Home

I
Far out on the dark river,
a fish jumps.

Dew is gathering on dry willow branches.

My friends lie asleep,
and I head back to our tents in the locust trees,
a mile away.

Inland,
the river has left a still pond.
A few snipe call back and forth in the night.
Their small tracks in the mud
	fill up with moonlit water.

I think of
anonymous Chinese poets, old poems on silk,
the pleasure of being alone,
walking
through a herd of cows asleep in scant alfalfa,
	the last crop of summer.

2
Over my head, the moon is half in the sky,
half in the locust branches.
Some people are still awake, talking softly.
Our small fire falls to a circle of quiet coals.

Falling asleep,
I trace the long drive home tomorrow; south—
        then west,
            across the mountains.
And someone has mentioned Seattle.

Garbage cans
spill over onto the sidewalk at Tai Tung,
        and the fat cook limps
            back through the screen door, smiling.

Down on the docks
they're unloading a boatful of black-eyed halibut.
A fisherman
seeing the moon on the wet deck
remembers Norway.

3
Along the Columbia,
        three more hours and I'm home.
But first
I close the car door
and walk in a field of mountain grass.

I lie down, drink
clear water, dream of old rituals
and what it feels to be pure of heart.

4

When I get back home to the Ish River country,
I'll open the barn door
and see the hides of white horses
        shedding rain.

Two Poems from Swede Hill

I
Barn

Suddenly there are ancient odors!
My grandfather's barn!
Pitchforks lean in the far corner,
prongs stuck in old planks.
A dim puddle of oil
    covered with hayseeds and dust
lies under the stored mowing machine.
Cobwebs stretch
between rusted tines of the pitchforks.
At the bottom of a dusty gallon jug,
its cork fallen in,
a mouse
lies on his back,
    twisted in his last breath,
    the unfinished
    gestures of life.

2
House

My grandmother,
for the joy of hearing the floor creak with
the mysterious feeling of damp cellars,
walks
over the kitchen floor.
Down there
a spider sleeps, legs folded together
making a witch's hand.
Listen: such silence gathers,
you hear
the generous orange squared heart of a fir beam
releasing a trickle of powder,
little grains falling to fleck the pale white long legs of
        old potatoes
reaching for their youth.

Just Before Sleep, I Dream of My Grandfather Returned to His Farm in the Early Spring

1

Where he stands
halfway out in the field, still as a tree,
he doesn't see me watching
from under a fenceline cedar.
His old clothes weigh heavy on him.
His eyes are hatching something new
        for the one big field
        that always worked him hardest.

Is he thinking tractors, not horses, now?
For in this field
he liked to tromp lopsided in a furrow
behind his horses,
"the best team of whites in Grays Harbor county,"
ploughing.

2

Where the drainage ditch once ran
before its cedar casings rotted
        —a trace of red in the mud—
        water
        lies on the grass

draining off so slow
the lightest grasses do not budge.

He knows everything there is
waiting to do.

3
When I slip through the fence,
      bend low over a wire—
a staple pulls out of a post
leaving two dark eyes in the wood.
The wire goes limp
      without a noise.

Alder saplings
no bigger than switches
have come into the field a year before me,
fervent with new leaves.

Standing in the shadow he casts
I am close enough to touch or speak to him.
But no word comes right enough.

4
In a corner of the woodshed near the house
patches of powdery mold
are spreading
over his work shoes.

My Father

1
In America, history goes by quickly.

Like a windstorm.

Finland
is a coat flattened against my father,
        like newspaper
        caught in blackberry.

2
I think of his grave
        in the small cemetery outside Elma,
name and dates
carved in the headstone.
I remember the day he was buried by greedy men.
And the day before:
my mother, my brother and his wife, and I,
upstairs in Whiteside's Funeral Parlor,
followed by the undertaker,
we walked across a lavender carpet
while the pastel lights
sent cheap violins weeping through the air,

trying to break us
between the rows of luxurious coffins.

My mother said, and almost laughed,
"shopping for a coffin,"
before she fell apart, crying in my arms,
trembling into her widowhood.

3
I said: "Dad hated this . . . Let's not let them
      beat him at the last."

That day we chose the cheapest coffin
      this country can make.
I watched the undertaker
wilt into his lavender economy and try to smile.
And my father
grew joyful inside me.

Back out on the street,
my brother shoved the car into second gear,
roaring, "This country
      has gone to hell!"

In the back seat, our mother sat quaking
and holding behind a handkerchief her destroyed mouth.
Over the craggy ridges of the handkerchief
her eyes burned shut
and cracked like ashes in the rain.

For My Brother, Don, at Porter Creek, in Late February

It is winter, the night wandering away.
And below the leaves that have lain so long in puddles
an unseen life calls
like a voice in a cavern; we are
      walking in,
      deeper,
the new light appears huge, light that was
visible in wings of dragonflies
on summer afternoons.

Travelers, hotel rooms,
remember them,
leaves filling up the branches, building
      the voice we can hear
        when we stand still next to our shadows.
"It will be
a beautiful spring."
I felt it tonight,
it was being prepared
inside the rose,
the silent shifting of ash in the petals,
in the trees,
in the earth between the waking roots,
the suck of rising water,

and I say
to my brother when he comes so easily to mind again
and I see him standing
on the river bank, steelheading,
the river below him like the swirling air in a chalice,
alone in the wind,
rain hissing where it falls at the edge of his fire:

    Wait.
    The blood that flows between us.
    The smile of your wife, your children,
    the hills behind your house,
    our father.
    Wait.
    I will be there with the sound of water,
    with the sound of ashes,
    with the whipped leaves of cottonwoods,
    with the still shadows of firs,
    wait,
    for I am drifting down through
    the clouded water of the Chehalis,
    to be there with you,
    standing
    among stones, and mud, and sticks, and pierced leaves,
    where we will see the pale silver side of a steelhead
    passing by, upstream,
    another winter gone,
    and you
    and me
    so much closer to our father,
    that river he has now become.

Stand there.
Wait for me.
I'm drifting, drifting down to greet you,
my brother.

On Christmas Eve in the Hospital,
My Mother Finds She Has an Enlarged Heart

We gathered, we came close
to reclaim kinship, that river
called Generosity
which sustains our family.
When she said
what the doctor had said,
in her eyes a bird flew over a field and
      dropped into the tall grass,
      terrified.

Because I now know
how we die daily of unexpressed affections,
I said:
      To us,
      it was nothing new; we'd always known
         she had a big heart.

Out of the sapped and withered grass then
the bird rose in her short flight.

There Is No Exile Where
the Heart Is Pure

(for Pablo Casals)

Behind the barn, the first week of March, on a bright
morning after long rain,
the windy cedar tree
turns round and round in the sunlight.
A winter horse
rubs himself on the corner of the barn.
Little pieces of cedar glide down where the ants are
calling home their old senators who
have failed utterly.

Coming home, carrying suitcases full of noise,
they pass through small American towns.

On the barn wall,
rusted nails bleed; and in fences, in hinges, in boards.
The horse (I think of Casals in exile!) plays
a suite unaccompanied in the silver cedar boards.
Inside the barn,
the stranded haywagon shudders.
Between its floorboards
seeds
trickle to the earth.

A dry dusty odor mingles with festering dampness,
and a hand—
        blue ridges and rivers coming and going through it—
rests on the white sheet of the windows.

        My grandmother
        comes to swing open wide the huge
        double doors,
        doors like drifting continents,
        and a wedge of healing sunlight
        slips into the barn before her.

Steelhead

The day I landed my first steelhead
from the Chehalis,
I saw a crow
zigzagging across Damitio's field
like no other crow has done before.

Answering, for My Brother

What do I do?
I show you barns in the air over Porter Creek.
Tulips that drop from trees in Venezuela
        and fall to the ground,
        bursting into roosters.
They whip the dust
out of small valleys under their wings.
Under the arches of their clawed feet
mountains blossom,
        distant but clear.

At the edge of ploughed fields
the surrounding sunflowers
march weary-hearted
heading into the cities of the sun.
Impossible not to follow them
and go with strange-shaped footsteps that
        might slowly turn bitter as green seeds.

Thin floating webs glide on the upper winds,
flash once or twice a dry silver fire,
then
        return to their invisible journey.

It is easy to see
        that among the insect world,
        many pilgrims have fallen to their knees.

Considering Poverty and Homelessness
(Homage to Bashō)

I cannot go back now,
      for what I have not done.
Of what is done,
take—and be kind.
      I am building a voice for my grief.
Alone, on foot,
if years from now I have learned anything,
      I will wander back.
Dust will rise up
on a dry winter road
where no one has walked before.

In Praise of My Ink Bottle

1

Life flows on, I go from place to place.
I carry this ink bottle with me
      wherever I go.

2

At the dinner table in some friends' house,
eating and drinking wine, I look down
and see the ink on my fingers.

Book 2

Stumbling Through Towns

Centuries Go By

In the world of men
centuries go by leaving
little trace.

A blossom in men is
like a cathedral,
seldom built.

It must be that in schools
when the blackboard is being erased,
under the sweeping hand,
    some words
    disappear forever.

Seattle in April,
Cloudy Day
and High Wind

(for Joseph Goldberg)

I
Along Seventeenth Avenue, the trees
hold down big handfuls of old green
light, and the spring-time
is fresh.

From an upstairs window—

> over the alley
> over the tops of houses
> over the power poles holding up the weight of
> > so many tangled electric lines,
>
> and over,
> in the next distance,
> maples of the University,
> over a church on Fifteenth,
> above the trashy adventure of men in commerce,

the endless clouds
glide grey and white above the city,
immense
and changing,

ocean wind bringing them in
over the Sound, over mountains and valleys.

These clouds bring no rain.
They are carried on
as blades of grass are carried in ditches
        while no one sees.

2
In the miles and miles
of this city there is no house for me.
I remember peaceful moments,
away—

Thirsty, I go out to buy a sack of beer,
come back, park the car,
step over a fallen twig of cherry heavy with blossoms,
        it is time to go.

I sit in a friend's third-floor room, looking out.
There's the noise of traffic
and construction, huge
        concrete walls lowered into place.
A sickening blindness in everything.

I spend the afternoon
looking closely at the map: roads and rivers, and
mountains.

I wonder what it's like in the town of

        Wildwood,
        Washington.

"Storm Sinks Greek Ship, 281 Perish"

December 8, 1966

(for George Hartwell)

I

Oh no,
I said. It was the word "perish"
that cut my breath, and
the water laden with so many bodies.
Windows and doors opened and closed.
A storm of leaves fell.
Strong hands held the door.

I tried to think of them, then,
    in the stormy Aegean,
      enroute from Crete to Piraeus.
Two hundred and eighty-one
floating
face down
flayed with salt water
one by one growing heavy
dropping
down
into the dark field below the wave,
below the table with bread and fruit,
below even the great whale,
invisible in the blackness
who watches for a long time

a foot, a thigh, a torn face, falling and
disappearing into the greater dark below him.

I thought of
cold. Of water in the lungs,
        the peaceful feeling they say that comes
        with the first stillness
        when the blood goes slack
        and the bones around the eyes fade away.
        And for those still living
        the body lies
        fallen,
        apple, branch, rag.

2

There was
"a crew of seventy-five commanded by
Captain E. Vernikos,
and two hundred and six passengers,
including one foreigner . . ."
"The foreigner was not immediately
identified."

The foreigner—
I might have stopped him on the street
as I did the postman today, to say
something absurd
about the weather, but
something that said there you are, and
here I am, it is winter, we
feel the snowy winds out of the mountains,
it is cold,
and we know that in the maple trees,

inside the buds at the tips of the black branches,
      there is long, long sleep.

3
When what is left of the foreigner—
      what fish and stranger creatures did not eat—
comes down at last
to the silent mud
where great treasures have lain,
      anchors of precious metal,
      chains,
      oar locks,
      stone jars that held
      grain, salted meat, and cool sweet water,
      companions of long journey,
down there
he nudges the mud in one place
to uncover the scarred metal, iron sword of Vikings,
touched for
the first time in thirteen hundred years.
Ending his fall,
he trips the leg bones of a fiddler,
      one of my ancestors, maybe,
      no sailor,
      who came along to see
      the white islands,
      the dark women walking with heavy jars on their heads,
the sun hot on his face,

the wind that crossed his ship,

his fiddle-bow that rode over the gut strings

    and made the song
    that brought him to lie songless
    in Mediterranean mud,
to perish . . .

East of the Mountains, Driving
to White Swan

June 29, 1969

1

The Yakima river valley
half an hour before the sun goes,
driving past farms
Sunnyside to Granger, and on, beyond Toppenish,
fieldrows of young beans, dark brown earth
sunlight on the sea of leaves over the darkening cornfields,
the hops growing up on high crossed sticks
     like ruins that disappeared
     leaving green arms
     clasped
     in the air.
I have a feeling anything will grow here; this earth
is rich
for everybody.
Small ditches filled with seeping water,
the land is peaceful.

On one farm, in fields of mint, between green rows,
white geese
are bent over like Chicanos
weeding the mint.

Now and then one stands up,
    looks off into space,
looking at something over the tops of cars,
over houses,
far off,
    blue clouds over the Cascades.

This is the longest valley in the world.

2
At White Swan, out
    beyond all the farms,
maybe a light every once in a while,
in the sage,
in dark ravines filled with willow brush,
under the newly risen
full moon,
    the night is like deep water.

3
I'm getting here late.
This is
    the first council fire in forty years—
    All the tribes of the Yakimas are gathering tonight,
anyone welcome.

Following cars,
red tail lights in the dust,
a bright chilly night,
three miles out cars are gathered in a field,
white canvas teepees in a huge circle,
booths selling popcorn and soft drinks,

the bone game, and
a dirt-floor dance hall with
bleachers three rows deep,
everybody hunched up in the cold,

four Indian girls dancing off to one side, wearing bright
headbands and soft leather boots,
old men sitting around a drum,
          eight of them,
calling for the next dance. The chief,
cowboy hat and braided hair, in the circle of
          seated drummers,
the face of a real Indian,
lifts the tilted bright silver microphone
          off his knees:
"It's a cold night, yes," he says.
"Dance and you won't feel it."

He starts to lift his drumstick, but
          picks up the microphone again:
"This is everybody's war dance!"
And the old drummers, dry and distant,
laugh a little and shift in their chairs.

4
Later six men
from another tribe
with a drum come to play and chant.

These old men,
          are they
          the last?

34

Out there in the arena some wear feathers
       and dance,
       bending low,
       the sun rising on their backs
       circled by
       bright colored trembling feathers.

Here on the benches we all wear the same clothes
and have no bells on our feet.

Monday Morning in Everett, Washington

I

Taking a walk in the early morning,
in Everett. Not the most
beautiful place in the world.
Beyond the low buildings of the college,
black fir trees,
and beyond the trees, smoke pouring
from the high stack of Weyerhaeuser's mill.
In the old days of this town
sheriff, deputies, and townsmen stood on the dock,
their guns concealed, while the ship Verona
     drifted toward them,
       its engines cut.
The townsmen lifted their rifles then,
and fired.
A few Wobblies—
     working men who wanted to make a Union—
fell off the ship like shot crows
into the slack water, oil and sawdust,
chips of fir bark.

2
It is still going on.
This town needs
a saint.
Saint Everett of the Sawmills.

Out of the stack, dirty smoke
flows up into the grey, overcast sky.
Like a gaffed fish in an eddy,
a cloud of blood streaming out of a rip
        in the silver skin.

Here among the buildings,
sad architects are on the loose everywhere.
There are so few beautiful houses.
The town
is a stranded ship, a museum.
The houses along these streets now
are dying.
There are hardly any flowers.

Isaiah said:
        It shall be as when a standard-bearer fainteth.

If the angels of good heart are going to come,
let them come now,
burning the body clean, leaving
in our rinsed hands some flowers, the grass underfoot,
and the tiny cathedrals of song
where birds sit hidden in bushes,
        in the last living space
        between houses that are dying.

Americans Thinking of Religion

It is
they think
a 1937 Plymouth rusting on a creekbank.
Blackberry vines crawl through the windows.
Fieldmice
inhabit the back seat.
One tilted front wheel is sunk in the creek.
Rainbow trout
swim around the wheel,
    or rest
    in the dark shadow of the hood:
"God's true children"
heading upstream.

Grey Afternoon in Seattle During
the Viet Nam War

This is what it's like here.

The kittens look up from the floor like calendars.

Across the street, the Jewish family
is thrashing about,
I wonder what they're up to today,
making a movie maybe.
A couple weeks ago she asked me, that nice
neurotic mother—
please sir if you wouldn't park your car right there
my son he likes to park there
you know the poor boy just came from Viet Nam last week
they stole his tape deck and all kinds of
tapes, the poor boy you know he didn't get very much
money the army you know what they're like
and he just got back he saved his money
he didn't have a chance
to listen to them yet.

I said, yes, I'd move my car,
"No hard feelings," she said,

and I went away shaking my head inside
thinking
Jesus H. Christ.

Two Poems Against the Logging Companies

I

Crown Zellerbach

"VIRGIN CEDAR"
This is not the tree ancient Aesop saw.
This is not the tree that was made into Spanish ships.
This is not the tall spirit the coastal Indian knew—
        Quinalt, Quilleute, Makah—
        they waited out heavy rain
        under cedar and fir,
        waited,
        felt that peace,
        what was there.
This is not that tree. No.

This is the tree that the saw went racing through
head to foot, deafening the ears of sawyers.
This is where an endless string of quiet days went,
        "shot to hell."

Men in
business suits
from Boston walked through
these tall woods with gold

watches ticking in
        their pockets.

2
Weyerhaeuser

Everyone knows
        about the rotten air of Everett, Washington.
Everyone knows
        how the fish go belly-up in the water.
But this town is a text Weyerhaeuser can't seem to read.
This is the book
that will close over their frail wings
and not open again.

Mean Dog on Country Road

Walking down from Harris's place on Grand Ridge,
singing aloud to trees on both sides of me,
I pass an ugly pink house
set in a little hollow below the road.
A police dog begins to bark, then
comes running through the junk-strewn yard,
and stops at the edge of the road.
As I pass along, whistling
and pretending that I'm not scared,
he leaps out into the road.
I will not look back.
The bark is close behind me when
a loud woman's voice roars from the house:
"Trouble, get down here! Trouble! You get down here!"
Bolting out of the eighteenth century,
Dr. Johnson flings open a second-story window
and leans forward, saying:
        "O excellently named creature!
          O most excellently named!"
One by one,
famous men step out from behind the trees,
to join me as I keep on walking,
each trying to outdo the other in brilliance.
I can't recall all the conversations,

but I believe you know them,
having perhaps been troubled yourself
on strange roads
that lead back to the city.

Spring in Ish River

I can hear the two robins
crying from an alder across the creek.
Above me,
in the vine maple, I see the nest.
I reach up and feel the four eggs lying lightly
among soft feathers.
I lift one egg out, lower my arm
slowly, and
stand still,
appalled: I see
the true shape of my hand.

Lament for the Ancient Holy Cities

In the lost valleys of a man's life
there is always
a small bird asleep,
sad creatures
alone at the edge of deep woods,
moving
like beads held in the hands of holy men,
        chanting endlessly.

A prayer waits.
A lonely warrior stands
        at the brink of morning.

Book 3

Love Poems

It Seemed Summer When Everything Bloomed in Santa Barbara

(for Susanna)

It seemed summer, everything
sang in its turn and blossomed with a name.
We, on a high cliff over the Pacific
outside a small house, the ocean air
scented by jack pines in moonlight,
phosphorous waves over dark sand,
and in the still space between breakers,
      Newly come to love, I sought for words.

We leaned on the porch railing,
faced one another, then turned shyly away.
I remember the tall plant
blooming on the rising cliff, and
how we stood silent, until at last
you said its name: "They call it
the century plant, just once
every twenty years it blooms."
      Newly come to love, we needed signs.

"It's slow," I said,
"born as love is,"
heaven-bent emissary
bearing a homely gift of blossoms at its crown.
Beyond these praises, how do you honor

so long a labor: twenty silent years?
      Newly come to love, we needed words.

Far below us in the light-enfolded waves,
a waking gull stretched its wings
and cried.
I heard you say: "speak of the gift,"
and answered: "consider the burden
of twenty human years, and then rejoice."
      Newly come to love, everything spoke to us.

Still as the winds
moving through the pines,
moonlight shone on your face.
You drifted away,
and I was thinking of wild mustard and daisies
at home in the North, how they came
every summer to ravish the fields unfailingly.
      Newly come to love, we fall to memory.

I will praise this shyest blossom
born only in the mind.
"It would have kept Cézanne awake all night,"
you said, ". . . and Berthe Morisot
would lift her brush to touch canvas."
Just then, we turned
face to face, I kissed you
and saw a stranger blossom in your eyes.
      Newly come to love, we find ourselves.

In the Woods above Issaquah

In the woods above Issaquah
near a grey farmhouse
we pick wild plums in the rain.
Another day, on Sauk Mountain,
we lie in a meadow. A bird
jolts a stalk of fireweed
so the light seeds drift over us
     and down the slope.
Far below, the Skagit River
winds toward the sea, turning
     like a pattern in old jade.
At home, you put some tomatoes
on the window sill to ripen,
and I think of jade again.
Nights,
while a bird outside the window
begins to budge the night away
     with a single sound,
your breasts, your lips, your eyelids
are delicate as petals of
     winter poppies.
I don't know what happened.
One night, no use knocking on your door.
I stepped down from the front porch

as rain fell through big leaves
and the grass woke up,
    and your face was
    a small round stone
    falling through dark water.

Sitting Alone at Night, Thinking of Old Promises

(Eleni)

At night by the river
I see you fling your arms up into the sky,
      the moon visible between them.
There are no roots growing from your feet,
you float away.

The limb of a flowering tree comes down over a
      high brick wall,
the tip of a branch rests
      like the prow of a ship on water,
and sails on so slowly that in the morning when birds wake up
in the garden,
and sing,
an old sea captain standing on deck
far out at sea
      turns his head
      as though he heard them singing.

While drops of water
glisten on the mast and on the bright deck,
he lifts his dead wife up
once more
into the meadows of his heart,
as one day the flattened grass

slowly lifted the shape of her body
into the air.

He is like a young man again,
saying:
>"Summer has come by like a ship of blossoms,
and if you call my name, I will
meet you—as I promised—
in the tall windows of the rose,
and hold you there, forever."

On This Side of the Mountains

On this side of the mountains, I found you,
and soon go back.
Tonight, shadows ripple over the coals,
and in me, your gift,
immense silence.
I hear a song I have placed my lips upon
for you alone.
I bring this old harp,
I unclothe it for you.

Over the mountains
ripening fields of wheat stand and wait,
and I have seen in you, suddenly,
your moon, your darkness,
and the sacrament they make together.
Because of your beautiful body,
and because you step
reluctantly into your nakedness,
I go like a white shadow
drifting through your darkness.

You are not alone,
and I have two hands.
I have made a home for you in my hands.

In one, a song.
In the other, someone far away
lies down and sees in mountain passes
a blue flower
lifting its green arms out of the snow.

"I will leave you to go there, but
not before I plant in your heart
the jewel of this night between us."

Pyrrha and Deucalion

They are given the prize of a child.
They have labored on the side of a far-off mountain.
Alone
Under pine trees,
She walks
On an autumn day,
The first of September,
The blueberries ripe.
When she thinks of Deucalion,
There are children close by
In the grass.
Farther up the mountain,
Out of stone,
Come blocks, for a home, or
        for a tower.

He sang frequently,
Low quiet songs.
Often a bird would be looking up at him,
He was so serene.
Watching the bird fly off down over the meadow,
Skimming the lavender blossoms of heather,
The fleabane, the fireweed, and the phlox,
He would see

Pyrrha
Coming up along the path.
Her walking made for him
An open window,
A song somewhere deep inside the house,
The scent of pine boughs on the table,
The wind in the night trees,
Her dress,
The sound of a small stream flowing
In the night between them.

Your Angels Go with Me Too

Your angels go with me too.
With so much of your gift mine,
why should I not return?
Whenever a feast is spread before you,
you touch the table. Your hands
turn the light inside them,
and hold it,
      like moonstone,
      like a flower.
Who was prepared for this—
Who was prepared for this!

The Widow

A mouse has climbed down
the wall, into
a coat
hanging on a nail,
into the sleeve.

The phrases
of love are long phrases.
Too long.

Two Seasons

1
Fall

What can I say to you?
A pheasant rises out of the grass,
     over the field
     into the dark trees,
         gone.

2
Winter

In the abandoned orchard, winter apples
hang black in the moonlight.
Three deer
nosing the snow for windfalls
move under the trees
preserving with each movement
the stillness
of this
windless night.

Spring Poem in the Skagit Valley

The birds are going the other way now,
passing houses as they go.

And geese fly
            back
        and forth
            across the valley,
            getting ready.

The sound of geese in the distance
        is wonderful:
            in our minds
            we rise up
            and move on.

Design by David Bullen
Typeset in Mergenthaler Bembo
by Wilsted & Taylor
Printed by Thomson-Shore
on acid-free paper